POKÉMON® READER

TOGEPI SPRINGS INTO ACTION!

Adapted by Tracey West

Scholastic Inc.

New York   Toronto   London   Auckland   Sydney
Mexico City   New Delhi   Hong Kong   Buenos Aires

ISBN 0-439-42991-9

12 11 10 9 8 7 6 5 4 3   3 4 5 6 7 8/0

Printed in the U.S.A.
First printing, February 2003

One spring day, Ash and his friends were taking a walk.

Misty's Togepi wiggled in her arms. "What is it, Togepi?" Misty asked.

A Pokémon ran right past them.
"It is a Houndoom!" Ash said.

The Houndoom ran off.

But the friends had another surprise.

"Look! There is Team Rocket!" Brock said.

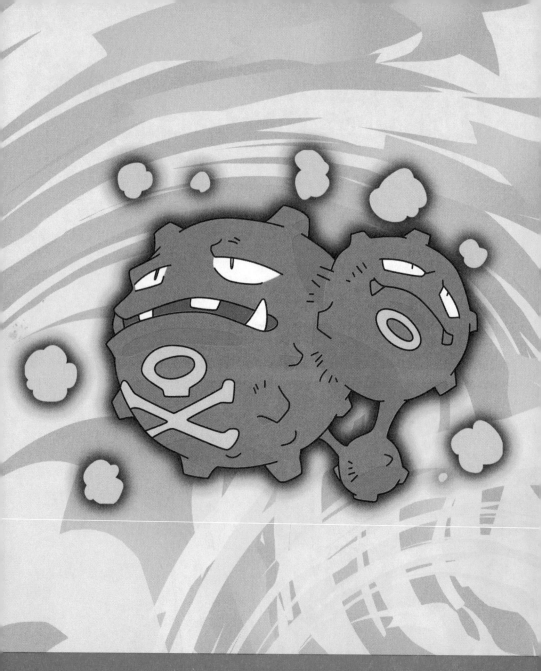

"We are here to catch Pikachu," said
Jessie.

James threw out a Poké Ball. "Go,
Weezing!" he cried.

Weezing used a Smoke Screen attack.

Misty could not see.

She fell down.

Then Togepi tumbled out of her arms!

Togepi rolled through the smoke.

The little Pokémon landed right in front of Weezing.

Togepi used Metronome.

Poof! Togepi vanished.

Pikachu slammed into Weezing.

Chikorita used Razor Leaf to break
Team Rocket's balloon.

"We are blasting off again!" cried
Team Rocket.

But Togepi was still in trouble.
The Metronome attack had put
Togepi high up in a tree.
Togepi started to cry.

Houndoom heard Togepi cry.
   It climbed up the tree.
   Then Houndoom carried Togepi to
the ground. Togepi was safe!

Houndoom went on its way.

Then Houndoom heard a noise.

Togepi was in trouble!

Houndoom turned around.
A Pinsir was attacking Togepi!

Houndoom ran as fast as it could.
Bam! It tackled Pinsir.
Togepi was safe again.

But the little Pokémon was lost and
alone.
Togepi started to cry again.

Houndoom could not leave Togepi all
alone.

    It picked up Togepi with its tail.

    Then Houndoom ran off through the
trees.

Meanwhile, Misty could not
find Togepi anywhere.
    "Noctowl can help us look,"
Ash said. "Go, Noctowl!"

Houndoom and Togepi were far away
from Misty.

Soon they came to a river.

To get across, Houndoom jumped
from rock to rock.

A Gyarados jumped out of the river!
Houndoom fell into the water.

Togepi
hung on as
Houndoom
swam to
the shore.

They made it!

Togepi and Houndoom climbed
up to a green field.

Ledyba flew above the flowers.

Three pretty Bellossom danced in the grass.

Togepi danced along with them.

The field was full of Grass and Bug
Pokémon.

But Houndoom had to keep going.

"Togi! Togi!" said Togepi as it waved
good-bye.

Not far away, Noctowl had found something.

"It looks like footprints," Ash said.

"They belong to Togepi!" Misty cried.

Ash, Misty, Brock, and Pikachu followed the footprints to the river.

They jumped from rock to rock.

Then they climbed up to the green field.

But Togepi was not there.

Houndoom and Togepi ran on and on.

Then it began to rain.

They found a dry spot under a tree.

Togepi's friends were not far behind.

Pikachu found more footprints.

They followed the footprints to the tree.

But Houndoom and Togepi had already left.

Houndoom and Togepi soon came to a Mareep ranch.

"There you are, Houndoom," said the rancher. "I see you have brought the supplies I needed — and a new friend, too!"

Togepi's friends finally caught up.

   "Togepi!" Misty cried. "I am so happy you are safe."

But things were not happy for long.
A net dropped from the sky and caught Houndoom!
The net belonged to Team Rocket!

"Chikorita, use Razor Leaf!" Ash yelled.
The sharp leaves cut through the net.
Houndoom was free!

"Houndoom, use Flamethrower!" yelled the rancher.

Houndoom blasted the balloon with fire.

"We are blasting off for the second time!" Team Rocket wailed.

Togepi hugged Houndoom.

   It was sad to leave its new friend.

   But it felt good to be back with its old friends, too.

   "Pika pika!" Pikachu thought so, too.